For Gma, Gpa, and all of their webby guests

First published in the United States of America in June 2018
by Bloomsbury Children's Books
www.bloomsbury.com

Bloomsbury is a registered trademark of Bloomsbury Publishing Plc

For information about permission to reproduce selections from this book, write to
Permissions, Bloomsbury Children's Books, 1385 Broadway, New York, New York 10018
Bloomsbury books may be purchased for business or promotional use. For information on bulk purchases please contact
Macmillan Corporate and Premium Sales Department at specialmarkets@macmillan.com

Library of Congress Cataloging-in-Publication Data
Names: Grant, Jacob, author, illustrator.
Title: Bear's scare / by Jacob Grant.
Description: New York : Bloomsbury, 2018.
Summary: Bear cares about keeping his house clean and tidy almost as much as he cares about his
stuffed friend, Ursa, so he is determined to find the spider building messy webs there.
Identifiers: LCCN 2017034048 (print) | LCCN 2017049593 (e-book)
ISBN 978-1-68119-720-3 (hardcover) • ISBN 978-1-68119-721-0 (e-book) • ISBN 978-1-68119-722-7 (e-PDF)
Subjects: | CYAC: Cleanliness—Fiction. | Bears—Fiction. | Spiders—Fiction. | Friendship—Fiction.
Classification: LCC PZ7.G7667574 Be 2018 (print) | LCC PZ7.G7667574 (e-book) | DDC [E]—dc23
LC record available at https://lccn.loc.gov/2017034048

Art drawn with charcoal and crayon then colored digitally
Book design by Jacob Grant and John Candell
Typeset in Brandon Grotesque
Printed in China by Leo Paper Products, Heshan, Guangdong
1 3 5 7 9 10 8 6 4 2

All papers used by Bloomsbury Publishing, Inc., are natural, recyclable products made from wood grown in well-managed forests.
The manufacturing processes conform to the environmental regulations of the country of origin.

Bear's Scare

JACOB GRANT

BLOOMSBURY
NEW YORK LONDON OXFORD NEW DELHI SYDNEY

Bear was sure of many things.

He was sure that his house was clean.
He was sure that his rooms were tidy.
He was certainly sure that he took very
good care of everything inside.

There was one thing Bear loved to care for most of all. A small stuffed friend, named Ursa.

They were always together.

Each day Bear and Ursa cleaned the house high and low. They cleaned inside and out. It was on such a day that Bear found something odd.

“That’s funny,” said Bear. “I am sure
I did not leave any books out.”

When Bear looked closer,
he saw something not funny at all.

Bear tried to keep calm, but the more he searched, the more messy webs he found.

"Ursa, we have a spider problem," said Bear.

"I am sure the spider is covering our home
with more sticky webs."

"I am sure the spider is making a giant mess with its many legs."

“I am certainly sure the spider is nothing like us,” said Bear.

“Ursa, we must find this messy guest.”

Bear and Ursa searched high and low.
They searched inside and out.

But they did not find any spiders.

"This spider is extra sneaky, but it cannot hide from us!" said Bear.

He sprang up to continue the search, when something terrible happened.

Bear lay there for some time.

"My poor friend. I sure never meant
to make such a mess."

Once again, Bear searched high and low.
He searched inside and out.

He had to find a way to help his friend.

When Bear returned he could not believe
what he saw.

His dear Ursa was good as new.

There among the books, Bear found
something he never expected.

He did not mind the spider's sticky webs.
He did not mind the spider's many legs.

"I certainly do not mind sharing my home with one more friend."

And that was something Bear could be sure of.